2334

$ **7.70**

W9-BMY-220

Adventures

of

Mohan

Adventures

of

Mohan

By Ella Grove

Artist: Edith Burkholder

Rod and Staff Publishers, Inc.
P.O. Box 3, 14193 Hwy. 172
Crockett, Kentucky 41413
Telephone: (606) 522-4348

Copyright 1990

By Ella Grove

Printed in U.S.A

ISBN 0-7399-0091-9

Catalog no. 2334

7   8   9   10   11   —   15   14   13   12   11   10   09   08   07   06

*With memories
of experiences shared
while in India with
ELMER,
my husband*

contents

1. Mohan and the Scarab 11
2. Mohan and Morgee 17
3. Mohan at the Market 23
4. Mohan Meets Marcus 31
5. Mohan's Birthday Surprise 39
6. Mohan Helps Father 45
7. Mohan Teaches Marcus 51
8. Brothers 63

9. *A Visit to the Jungle* 69

10. *At the Seashore* 79

11. *An Early Morning Walk* 87

12. *Bringing Home the Buffalo* 95

13. *The Monsoons Arrive* 101

14. *Planting Rice* 107

15. *Mohan and the Goat Herder* 113

16. *Mohan Goes to School* 121

17. *The Telltale Trail* 127

18. *Uncle Purno* 135

   Glossary of Pronunciations and

      Definitions 142

1.

Mohan and the Scarab

"Time to wake up, Mohan (Mō′ han)," Mother called as she went to the straw mat and shook the little boy, who was sleeping soundly. "Come quickly," she told him. "This is the day we go to the river to wash the clothes."

Mohan stood up and stretched his arms high above his head, as if he were trying to reach the chickens that had slept on the ledge above him. He yawned and rubbed his eyes.

"It is time for us to be going," Mother said as she scooped some rice into Mohan's tiffan (tif′ fən). Then she gathered the towels, sheets, and Mohan's shirts, and they started for the river.

"Mohan, you sit on the riverbank and eat your rice while I go into the stream to that rock that is sticking out of the water," Mother told him.

Mother set her bundle of wash on the rock and

rubbed and scrubbed a shirt with a cake of blue soap. She swung the shirt over her head and hit it smartly on the stone several times. Then she rinsed it in clean water.

"I'm coming, Mother," Mohan called when he had finished his rice.

Mohan skipped to the place in the river where his mother was working. The water was higher than Mohan's knees. He giggled and splashed.

"Look, Mother, there go some fish." Mohan plunged into the water after them and got his clothes all wet.

Mother caught him and rubbed him with soap. She ducked him into the water to rinse him off. It was a quick bath, and the warm sun soon dried his clothes again.

Mohan's work was to spread the clean, wet clothes on the grass to dry. He ran up the riverbank, and was ready to spread out the towels when he saw something that made him take two steps backward. He looked again, then squatted on his heels like all Indians do. He giggled.

"Mother, come quickly," he called. "Here is the funniest thing in the whole world."

Mother came, bringing a freshly washed sheet to spread out to dry.

"What are you seeing?" she asked.

Mohan giggled again and said, "Two bugs are

trying to roll a ball, and they are pushing it up the hill with their hind feet. How can they push it? Where did they get the ball? What will they do with it?'' Mohan asked his questions all at once, not giving Mother a chance to answer him or to get a word in edgewise.

"Those bugs are scarabs (scar′ əbz), Mohan,'' Mother told him. "They are also known as manure beetles. What did I say they are called?'' she asked him.

"Scabs,'' Mohan said quickly.

Mother laughed. "No, no. It's scarab. Try to remember the name to tell Father. Some people call them tumblebugs because sometimes when they are trying to push a ball uphill they lose their balance and roll over.''

"Where did they get the ball?'' Mohan asked next.

"They made it. They rolled mud and cow manure together, and now they are trying to take it to their home in the ground. They will lay eggs in it from which will hatch little bugs. The baby bugs will eat the ball when they get hungry,'' Mother explained to him.

"The manure ball is as big as my fist,'' Mohan observed, "and the scabs—I mean scrabs—I mean *scarabs* are the size of Father's big toe.

"There it is rolling down again,'' Mohan

shouted in excitement. "Now they are both behind it, pushing. Hurrah! They got it all the way to the top. It is rolling faster!

"Where is it now?" he asked, perplexed. Then he answered his own question. "Oh, there is a hole, and it must have gone down. How hard they worked, but they got it done," he concluded.

"Nothing is wasted in our country," Mohan told Mother later. "Even manure is used to feed the baby bugs."

Mother agreed and then added, "The sun is warm, Mohan, and the clothes have dried already. Come, we shall gather them up and go home. You must tell Father about the tumblebug scarabs."

2.

Mohan and Morgee

Ur-ur-aroo! called Moorga (Mōōr′ gä) one morning.

Mohan rolled over on his straw mat and yawned.

Ur-ur-aroo! Moorga called again and flapped his wings.

This time Mohan opened his eyes. There stood Moorga, the rooster, looking at him as if to say, "Wake up, sleepyhead."

Then the other chickens came running to Mohan.

"Good morning, Baboo (Bä bōō′). Good morning, Barda (Bär′ da) Baboo and Chota (Chō′ ta) Baboo and Moorgee (Mōōr′ gee)," Mohan greeted each one.

"Mother, is the rice ready for the chickens?" Mohan called to Mother, who was sitting outside with the supa (sū′ pä), cleaning rice for the day.

"I have some ready," Mother told him.

Mohan went to Mother. He gathered the broken grains of rice that Mother had sorted. "Chick, chick, chick," he called.

The chickens came running out of the house to the yard where Mohan threw the rice on the ground. What a hurry and scurry there was because Mr. Crow was saying, *Caw, caw,* and was flying low, watching for his chance to steal some rice.

"I will bring a pan of water for the chickens," Mohan said, and ran to the big clay pot where the water was stored.

After a while there was a sound like *Ca-ca-ca-ca-ak* coming from the box in the house. Mohan checked, and sure enough, Baboo had laid an egg.

Next it was Chota Baboo's turn to say, *Ca-ca-ca-ca-ak.* She too had laid an egg.

Soon Barda Baboo was saying, *Ca-ca-ca-ca-ak,* and there was another egg.

The next time Mohan looked at the box, there sat Moorgee. He went over close to her and she only said, *Aaarrrk,* and pecked at him.

"Well, Moorgee, what's the matter with you?" Mohan asked. Then he added with a laugh, "Did you get up on the wrong side of the bed this morning?"

Moorgee only shut her eyes and stayed sitting on the eggs.

All day Moorgee sat there.

In the evening Mother said, "I believe Moorgee wants to be a setting hen. Let us put more eggs under her and see how she likes that."

Mohan helped count nine more eggs to slip under Moorgee's wings.

"How many does that make, Mother?" Mohan asked.

Mother held up her fingers and started Mohan counting. "One, two, three, four, five, six, seven, eight, nine, ten, eleven, twelve."

"Now, Mohan, we must leave her alone. We will fix another box where the other hens can lay their eggs," Mother told him.

Day after day Moorgee sat on the eggs, only getting off long enough to eat rice in the morning and to take a drink of clean water.

When she was off the nest, Mohan would go quietly and look at the eggs. "They look the same as the day we put them in the box," he told Mother.

One morning when Moorgee was outside eating rice, Mohan heard a little *peck, peck, peck,* coming from her nest. He ran over and looked, and there were some cracks showing on an egg.

"Mother," he whispered, "the eggs are cracking."

Mother hurried over. Soon one egg broke in half and a little yellow ball came out. It rolled over and soon was standing on two little legs. Its eyes opened

up, and the first thing it said was *peep, peep, peep.*

Mohan could hardly stand still and keep from shouting, but he clapped his hand over his mouth. His eyes got bigger and bigger.

Moorgee came back and flew up into the box. She looked at the little yellow ball that said, *Peep, peep.* Then she took her beak, tucked him under her wing, and sat on the nest.

The next morning when Moorgee got off the nest for her rice, there were twelve little yellow balls of fluff, all saying, *Peep, peep, peep, peep, peep.* Mohan was so happy he clapped his hands for joy.

"We will set these baby chicks outside beside Moorgee," Mother told him. "She does not need to sit on the nest anymore."

Mohan carefully lifted one little ball in each hand and carried them outside. Then he came back for two more, and then for two more until all twelve were following Moorgee and pecking here and there at little grains of rice.

Caw, caw, caw, screeched Mr. Crow from the top of Mohan's house. He was curious to know what those little yellow balls were and was also anxious to taste them.

Cluck, cluck, cluck, said Moorgee, and quickly the little chicks hid under her wings. She covered them up until Mr. Crow flew away.

Mohan watched for a long while. Then one little

yellow head popped up from under a wing and then another and another. They all looked at Mohan and said, *Peep, peep, peep.*

3.

Mohan at the Market

"Would you like to go to the market with me today?" Mother asked Mohan when the sun was just waking up.

"Yes, yes, yes, please," Mohan replied, jumping up and down for joy.

"You need a new shirt, Mohan, for when you will start to school," Mother told him. "But it takes rupees (ro͞o′ pēz) for a shirt, and we don't have. many."

Mohan thought and thought, and then he had an idea.

"Maybe we could sell one of the squash that is on the roof of the house," he suggested. "Would that give enough rupees for a shirt?"

"That is a good idea," Mother replied. "But how can we get it down?"

"I will climb up and cut it. Then it will roll down

for you to catch,'' Mohan answered.

Mother lifted Mohan up as high as she could, and he climbed to the top of the house. He was not very heavy, so his feet did not go through the thatch. He looked at all the squash, and when he found the biggest one, he took his little knife and carefully cut the stem.

''Here it comes,'' he called.

Brrrrrrr. The squash rolled down the roof and right into Mother's arms.

Mother had twelve eggs that she put into a small basket for Mohan to carry. She put rice in the tiffan. Mother carried the squash and a folded sheet in a large flat basket on her head, and they started down the road for market.

''Look at the pretty bird, Mother. What kind is it? Do you hear it whistle?'' Mohan asked as he pointed to a gray bird with green feathers on its head.

''It is called a barber bird because its tail looks like the open scissors that a barber has in his hand when he works at his job,'' Mother explained to him.

They walked quickly and Mohan's legs got tired, but he tried to keep up with Mother.

''I see the marketplace,'' Mohan exclaimed. ''See all the people going through that gate, carrying big loads on their heads.''

Soon Mother and Mohan were going in through

the gate too. Already there were rows and rows of people with sheets spread out on the ground in front of them on which were things to sell.

"Mother," Mohan exclaimed, "look at all the tomatoes, the green coconuts, and the cauliflower! There are custard apples! Oh, how I like custard apples!" Mohan saw so many good things that he could not talk fast enough to tell about them all.

"Here is a place for us to sit and sell our squash," Mother decided. She got out the sheet and spread it on the ground. Next, she cut the squash into eight pieces because it was very large.   .

"I will take out the seeds," Mohan offered. He carefully picked the seeds from the squash and spread them in the basket to dry. He and Mother would eat them on the way home.

Soon a lady came along and stopped in front of them. She looked at the squash. "How much for a piece of your big squash?" she asked.

"Two rupees, only two," Mother answered.

"I will take one. How much for the eggs?" she asked.

"One rupee each," Mother replied.

The woman took three eggs.

Already they had five rupees. Mohan could hardly wait until all the squash and eggs were sold. While they waited they opened the tiffan and ate their rice.

Mohan at the Market

"Just one more piece of squash to sell," Mohan said soon. "And the eggs are all gone. Will there be enough rupees for a new shirt, Mother?" he asked anxiously.

"Yes, Son. Here comes someone for the last piece of squash," Mother replied.

Mohan and Mother gathered up the sheet and went to the man who sold the shirt material.

"I will take one metre (mē′ tər) of this blue material," Mother told the man.

Mother gave the man ten rupees; then she and Mohan hurried along to find a tailor. A tailor is a man who has a sewing machine to make clothes.

"There are the tailors, Mother," Mohan said. He took Mother by the skirt and led her over to the row of sewing machines. A man was busily sewing at each machine.

"Could someone sew a shirt for me today?" Mother asked.

"I will," a young man answered.

The young man brought his tape measure and put it around Mohan's chest. He put it from his neck to his waist. Then he measured the length of Mohan's arm.

"It will take me one hour to make the shirt," the tailor said.

Mother gave the tailor the material. Now she and Mohan had time to walk around and look at all

the food, flowers, kettles, baskets, dishes, and spices in the market. The hour was almost gone when they came to a pile of green coconuts.

"How about a drink of coconut milk?" the man

asked Mother.

"That would surely be good," Mohan thought. He hoped and hoped Mother would think so too.

"Yes, we would like that very much," Mother replied.

The man took a sharp, curved knife. He cut the ends off two coconuts. He handed one to Mohan and one to Mother.

Mother and Mohan tipped the coconuts above their mouths and let the sweet juice run into their mouths. It tasted so good that Mohan just took little sips to make his last longer.

Mother paid the coconut man, and they hurried over to the tailor. He had Mohan's shirt finished.

On the way home, Mohan said, "This was a good day, Mother, but it will be good to be at home again because I am so tired."

"Yes," Mother replied. "It was a good day. We were able to sell the squash and the eggs and get a new shirt for you. There are still enough rupees left to buy you a new slate for school."

4.

Mohan Meets Marcus

"Good morning," someone called to Mohan from the gate.

Mohan turned around quickly. There stood a man Mohan had never seen before. He was tall and had white skin. Mohan stared. People with white skin were not often seen in his country.

Mohan ran to the door and called, "Mother, come quickly."

Mother set down her supa and hurried to the gate with Mohan.

"Good morning, sir." Mother spoke kindly to the stranger.

"My name is David," the man told her. "I have just come from North America to help your neighbor, Brother John, bring good news to your village. My wife has come, and also Marcus, our son. I think he would be the age of your son."

"This is Mohan, my son," Mother introduced him. "He is five, running six."

"Yes, yes," the man said. "Marcus too will be six next month. I shall send him over to meet Mohan."

Mohan could hardly wait to meet Marcus. After lunch he heard someone call from the gate. He hurried out to see who was there.

"Are you Marcus?" he asked the boy at the gate.

"Yes," Marcus replied. "Father told me about you and said that I may come and see you."

"Certainly, come in. I surely am happy to meet you. Do you like our country?" Mohan asked him.

"Yes, very much," came Marcus's reply. "I like your big trains. When we came here, we rode on a big, long train. There were hundreds of people on the train.

"When we stopped at a station, we heard cups rattling and it sounded to us as though the people were calling, 'Good-bye. Good-bye' to the folks on the train. Someone told me that instead of, 'Good-bye,' like I thought, they were saying, 'Garum Chai,' (Gər əm Chä′ ē) which you know means 'hot tea.' "

"I have never seen a train," Mohan said. "Could you tell me what one looks like?"

"I could try," Marcus answered. "There is a

big engine like a big strong bus and it pulls forty
or fifty train cars or bogies. They are like big buses
too.''

"Oh, I wish I could see one. But maybe someday I will be able to ride on one.'' Mohan gave a
wishful sigh.

"We had a ride on a rickshaw (rik′ shô),''
Marcus told him.

"I know what rickshaws are like.'' Mohan
beamed. "They are like bicycles with three wheels.
They have a wide seat for two people. There is a
roof over the top. Men pedal them fast, taking people
here and there. I like rickshaw rides. My Uncle
Rojen (Rä′ jən) has one, and he gets lots of rupees
for taking people for rides.''

"Tomorrow morning we are having Sunday
school in our house because Brother John is not well.
Do you think you could come?'' Marcus asked.

"I hope so,'' Mohan said, "but I cannot read
yet.''

"You do not need to read; you just need to sit
still and listen,'' Marcus told him.

"I can listen, but I have trouble sitting still,''
Mohan replied. "But I will try if Mother lets me
come.''

"I must go home now. I'm so glad to have met
you. You are my first friend in India. I hope to see
you in the morning.'' Marcus ran off to his house.

Mohan hurried in to Mother. "Oh, Mother. Marcus asked me to go to Sunday school at his house tomorrow. May I please, Mother? May I please? He said Sunday school will be at his house because Brother John is sick." Mohan coaxed.

"I will need to ask Father," Mother told him. "But wash your hands now because supper is ready."

Mohan slept on his straw mat and dreamed that he saw rows and rows of boys and girls with shiny brown faces all wearing clean clothes, going to Marcus's house.

Sunday morning Mohan awoke when Moorga, the rooster, crowed beside him.

"Is this the day I go to Sunday school at Marcus's house?" Mohan asked, almost before his eyes were open.

"Yes, Father said you may go," Mother told him. "Run quickly to the river for your bath. Don't forget to brush your teeth."

Mohan ran to the river and splashed in the cold water. When he returned, Mother had his new shirt all ready for him and a bowl of rice waiting. Quickly he ate his bowl of rice.

"Good-bye, Mother," he called as he hurried off to Marcus's house.

Soon some of his other friends began coming. There was Sosan (Sō′ sän), Mahesh (Mə hāsh′), and

Jay Prakash (Jī‑ē Prä käsh'). Then came Binode (Bi nōd') and Nehru (Nē hə rū').

Marcus's father spread out straw mats, and the boys sat down in a row.

"Good morning, boys," Marcus's father began. "My name is Brother David. I am happy to have you come to our house for Sunday school today. We want to begin by learning a little song. It goes like this:

> God is so good;
> God is so good;
> God is so good;
> He's so good to me.

"Now everybody help, and we will sing it together."

Mohan remembered most of the words and helped to sing the song.

"That was very good," Brother David said. "Let us sing it one more time. Everybody together!"

By now, Mohan knew all the words and the tune also.

Next, Brother David told the story of how Baby Jesus came from heaven to be the Saviour of the world.

"Now, let us pray a prayer," Brother David said. He began, "Dear Father in heaven, bless these boys. Please help them to remember the story and the song. In Jesus' Name. Amen.

"Please ask your fathers and mothers to come with you next Sunday to learn about the Bible, which is God's Word."

Mohan could hardly wait to get to his house to tell Mother and Father about the Sunday school at Marcus's house. He ran as fast as he could.

"We learned a nice song," he told them. "I can sing it for you. It is:

> God is so good;
> God is so good;
> God is so good;
> He's so good to me.

"Then Brother David told us a story from the Bible about Baby Jesus. He also said fathers and mothers should come along next Sunday and learn from the Bible. Will you please come along? Will you, please?"

"Yes, we will go with you next Sunday," Father promised Mohan. "We want to learn about God's Word."

5.

Mohan's

Birthday Surprise

Ur-ur-aroo! Ur-ur-aroo! crowed Moorga right by Mohan's head.

Mohan opened his eyes and smiled. "What are you saying, Moorga?" he asked. "It sounds like, 'Happy birthday to you.' "

Moorga flapped his wings and said it again. *Ur-ur-aroo!*

"Listen, Mother," Mohan called. "Is Moorga saying, 'happy birthday' to me?"

"That's what he says every morning, Son," Mother told him. "I'm sure he doesn't know that today is a special day; but I know it is your birthday."

"Am I really six years old now?" Mohan asked. "I have waited so long to be six. When may I start to school?"

"You will go to school when the next term

begins,'' Mother told him.

"I can hardly wait, Mother,'' Mohan added. He ate his bowl of rice and went outside to play.

"Good morning, Mohan. Is this your birthday?'' There was Marcus coming toward the gate.

"Yes. I am six years old today.''

"I came over to tell you I saw an elephant coming down the street, and it seemed to be stopping at every house,'' Marcus exclaimed excitedly.

"Oh, good!'' Mohan said. "I hope he keeps coming this way. I like to watch elephants. They are so big the ground almost shakes when they walk. Mother, Mother,'' Mohan called. "Marcus told me there is an elephant coming into our village and stopping at every house!''

"The elephant will be begging for its owner,'' Mother explained. "The owner sits on the elephant's back, and they stop at every house. The elephant holds out his trunk. People put a coin or banana or other food into the trunk. Then the elephant reaches it up to the man on top.''

"I have never seen anything like that,'' Marcus said.

Mother smiled a little smile. She was getting an idea. She hoped the elephant would stop at their house.

Mohan and Marcus stood at the gate, watching as the elephant came slowly down the street.

"There he is stopping at Sosan's house," Mohan said.

"Now he is coming to the next one," Marcus added.

"I wish he would hurry and get here." As usual, Mohan could hardly wait.

"I had better see if Mother has something to give him," Mohan said next. "Let's go in and ask her."

The boys hurried to the door. "Do we have something for the elephant?" Mohan asked.

"I will give him some rice in a little bag and also a rupee," Mother told them.

"Will the elephant eat the rice?" Marcus asked.

"He is trained to give the things to his owner," Mother answered.

"What do elephants eat?" Marcus wondered.

"They eat leaves and grass," Mother told him. "They wrap the end of their trunks around clumps of grass and tear them off. Then they curl up their trunks and put the grass into their mouths."

The boys ran back to the gate.

"He is almost here," they both shouted at one time.

The next minute the elephant was standing outside the gate with his trunk stretched out between the two boys.

They backed away. "It looks like a snake," Marcus whispered.

Mother came out and put a little bag of rice on the elephant's trunk. Up it went. The man on the elephant's back caught it.

"Just a minute," Mother called to the man. She opened the gate and said something quietly to him.

Immediately the man tapped the elephant's ribs with his stick. The elephant kneeled down on all four knees.

"The man will give you boys a ride on his elephant if you would like to go," Mother told them.

"That will be fun," they answered together.

The man held his stick down to the boys. "Hold on to my stick and walk up over the elephant's trunk and head," he instructed Mohan.

Mohan's legs shook a little, but up he went.

"Now it is your turn," the man said as he held his stick for Marcus.

"Whew, that was a long way up," Marcus said when he reached the top. "It almost seems like we are up in the trees."

The man tapped the elephant again and he stood up.

The boys rocked from one side to the other when the elephant walked, but his back was so wide that there was little danger that they would fall.

"What is the elephant's name?" Mohan asked the driver.

"His name is Jumbo because he is so big," came

the answer.

"How much does he weigh?" Marcus asked next.

"He weighs about four or five tons," the man told him.

"I wouldn't want him to step on my toe," Marcus decided.

"When he was a baby, he weighed one hundred and fifty pounds," the man explained. "Now he is forty years old, and he weighs several tons."

They went up the street as far as Marcus's house.

"Mother!" called Marcus.

Marcus's mother came running outside the house.

Marcus waved and said, "We are away up here."

Then they turned around and went back to Mohan's house. Again, the driver tapped Jumbo's ribs, and he kneeled down.

"Thank you very much," the boys told the man.

Holding on to the stick, the boys slid down the elephant's head and trunk.

Before Jumbo left, Mother put a rupee in his trunk. Up it went, right into the driver's hand.

"Mother," Mohan said, "that was the best birthday surprise a boy could have when he turns six years old."

6.

Mohan Helps Father

"Mother, may I go out to the field to see how Father is getting along with the plowing?" Mohan asked Mother one day.

"That would be very nice," Mother told him. "Why not take him something to drink. Here is the water from cooking rice. Father would like to drink that."

Off went Mohan. He hurried down the street and took the path through the mango (mang' gō) orchard.

"Those mangoes look so good," Mohan said to himself. "I just wish they would hurry and get ripe." Mohan always wanted things and people to hurry. Sometimes Mother called him, "Hurry-Scurry."

All of a sudden Mohan heard *plop!*

"Well now! What is that?" he asked himself.

Then there was another *plop* right in front of

him.

"Those are mangoes coming down, and each has a bite taken out of it," Mohan said.

Then Mohan heard some chattering in the tree right over his head. He looked up, and there sat two little monkeys looking down at him and grinning.

"You funny little fellows," Mohan scolded. "You are being naughty—picking the mangoes before they are ripe." He clapped his hands to scare them away.

They shrieked and chased each other, swinging from one branch to the next. Finally, they jumped to the ground.

"Good for you," Mohan told them.

The monkeys started running and again scurried up into a tree. As Mohan was walking on to find his father, there was another *plop*. This time it was not on the ground. A mango landed on his head.

Ha, ha, Mohan thought he heard the monkeys laugh.

Mohan came to the river. The water felt nice and cool to his bare feet. He stood in a sandy place and let the water roll over his toes. Then he waded across the river at a shallow place and climbed the bank on the other side.

"There is Father still ploughing," he said. Mohan hurried along the path.

"Father," he called, "I brought you a drink.

You must be thirsty.''

"It has been very warm," Father told him. "The buffaloes are getting hot and tired. They will be glad when we are through here so that they can have a bath.''

"How long will it be until you are finished?'' Mohan asked. "I would like to watch when you wash the buffaloes.''

"When the sun is straight above our heads and there are no shadows on any side of us," Father explained. "It will take about thirty minutes yet.''

"I will sit here and watch the birds," Mohan told Father. "The monkeys are into the mangoes,'' he continued, "and they dropped one on my head. It didn't hurt much, but I surely wish they would leave the mangoes alone.''

Mohan sat in the shade to wait. Back and forth went the buffaloes while Father followed them with the plow.

Father kept saying, "Birch, birch, birch'' which meant turn, turn, turn.

All of a sudden, Mohan heard, *Whir-r*. He looked up into the tree. There was a flock of wild parrots, which had just flown in.

As Father finished ploughing and drove the buffaloes from the field, Mohan looked up into the sky. "It must be twelve o'clock," he told Father. "There are no shadows around me at all. I must be standing on my shadow, but my shadow doesn't seem to mind.''

"Rich people have watches on their arms," Father explained, "but we use God's clock."

"Which is that?" Mohan asked.

"That is the sun," Father told him. "Only on cloudy days we are sometimes late for dinner. Come, now, it is bath time for the buffaloes. They have worked hard all morning, and they are very hot."

When the buffaloes saw the river, they started to run. They splashed into the water until their backs were covered and only their faces were out.

Father picked up Mohan, carried him into the river, and set him on Rao's (Rä′ ō) back.

"This is fun," Mohan told Father. "It makes me think of the elephant ride I had."

Mohan took his hands and rubbed Rao's face and ears. Then with his feet, he scrubbed his back.

Next it was Munci's (mən′ sē) turn.

"Time to go home," Father said, "but these fellows like the water so well that they wish I would leave them here all day."

"Birch, birch, birch," said Father.

Slowly Rao started for the edge of the river, and slower still came Munci.

As they walked up the path toward home, Mohan said, "Yum, yum. I think Mother has fixed a good curry to have with the rice today, and I am ready to help eat it."

7.

Mohan Teaches Marcus

"Good," Mohan said when he went outside one fine morning. "Feel that breeze! This is the day to fly kites. Mother, may I fly my kite today? Mother, may I, please?"

"Yes, here it is," she told him.

Up, up, up the kite went, right to the end of the string. Mohan held the string tightly so that it would not go up to the sky.

"Good morning, Mohan." It was Marcus coming down the street. "That looks like fun, but I do not know how to fly a kite. Where do you buy them?" he asked.

"We do not buy them. We make our own," Mohan told him. Then he added, "I will show you how. We can make one in a short time."

"Would you be so kind?" Marcus asked. "Then we could each fly one. What materials do we need?

I can run home and bring them.''

"We need newspaper, palm veins (the same as mothers use to make brooms), string, and cooked rice," Mohan told him.

"I'll be back as soon as I can." Marcus ran home repeating, "Paper, sticks, string, and rice. Paper, sticks, string, and rice. Paper, sticks, paper, ricks, string, and stice. Paper, stricks, sing, and strice. I wonder why we need rice."

In a few minutes Marcus was back at the gate. "I have paper, sticks, string, and rice," he told Mohan. "Did I forget anything?"

"No," Mohan said. "You remembered everything. It really doesn't take many different things to make a kite—only paper, sticks, string, and rice.

"Now we are ready to start," he instructed, just like a grown-up teacher would begin. "First of all, take the newspaper and fold it down this way to make a square. Now fold up the bottom section. Next, with a piece of this string, cut the extra paper off the bottom. Keep the paper you cut off; we will need it later."

"Now I have a square of paper." Marcus held it up.

"Are you ready for the next part?" Teacher Mohan asked.

"Yes, sir, I am ready," replied Marcus. Then

he thought, "This is almost like playing school."

"Now, please, take the piece of paper you cut off when making the square," Mohan directed.

"Here it is, sir," Marcus answered.

"Now divide that into five small pieces," commanded the teacher.

"Shall I use the string to cut them?" Marcus asked.

"That will make a nice, straight edge," Teacher replied. "Sometimes if we are in a hurry we tear them, but we should do this one neatly, especially for your parents to see.

Kite-making Directions

1. Fold newspaper on fold 1 to make square Ⓐ.

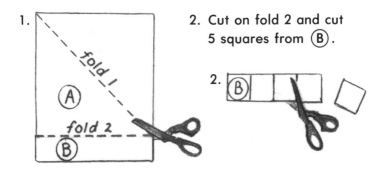

2. Cut on fold 2 and cut 5 squares from Ⓑ.

"Now we are ready for the sticks. First, put one stick from one corner to the opposite corner of the big, square piece of paper. Next, take one of the small squares of paper. Take a couple of kernels of cooked rice and rub them over the square, crushing them and smearing them over the paper with your fingers. That is the glue. Press the square over the stick at the top and fold the outside edges down. That makes it nice and strong."

"This is easy to do. What comes next?" Marcus asked.

"We take the other stick, which should be the same length as the first one. Tie each end of a string (that is the same length as the stick) to the ends of the stick. This will make it look like a bow for

3. Place 1 stick from corner to corner of large square Ⓐ.

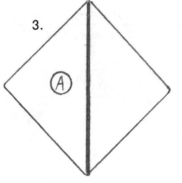

3.

Sticks should be ¼" square or round.

4. Press one small square (smeared with cooked rice glue) at top, gluing stick to paper.

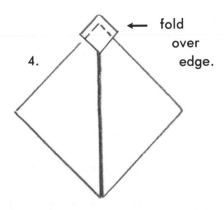

4.

← fold over edge.

5. Make second stick same length as the first. Tie string at both ends to make it bow.

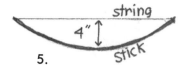

string

4"

stick

5.

notch stick ends →

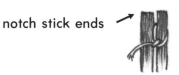

shooting arrows. I will help wrap the string around
the ends and tie them.''

The teacher tied the ends tightly.

''Now we are ready to put the 'bow' in place.
Lay it so that the string goes to the remaining corners
of the square and the stick toward the top. Put one
foot on each end where the string is tied to the stick,
and I will tie the pieces of wood together where they
cross each other.

6. Place second stick from corner to corner. Fasten second stick to first, with
   paper square gluing second stick to
   first exactly in the middle, allowing
   string to make kite bow.

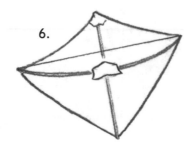

"Now we are ready for four more small paper squares. Smear them with rice glue. Put one square where your left foot is standing, to cover the stick and string. That is right. Now do the same where your other foot is standing. Next, put one glued square where the string crosses the stick, and one below it where the sticks cross.

"We are now ready to put the tail on the bird. We need long, narrow strips of paper, about so wide. I will help you to cut them," Mohan said. "Fold the paper over, and we will use the string

7. Press three more squares, one at each end of bowed stick, and one halfway between square on bowed stick and top of kite.

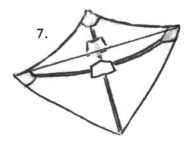

again to cut it. We should have three long pieces. We will glue them together with rice. After that we will glue the paper strip to the tail end of the kite.''

The boys worked in silence.

''Now for the last part,'' Teacher Mohan said.

''What is that?'' asked Marcus.

''We need to fasten strings to the kite so that we can hold it,'' Mohan instructed. ''Take a stick and punch two holes in the square that covers the point where the two sticks cross. On the square below the string, punch two holes also, one on either side of the stick.''

Marcus carefully followed the instructions.

''Next, take a double string about this long.'' Mohan held his hands about twelve inches apart. ''Thread it through one of the front holes from the bottom up, over the stick, and down again through the other hole.''

''I can hardly wait,'' Marcus said as he worked with the string. ''Do you really think it will fly?''

''I don't know why not, if we get a good breeze,'' Mohan told him. ''But we had better finish it, or I know for sure it won't fly.

''Now take a long string and double it so that the double string will be a little longer than the first string. Put it through the patch of paper that covers the bow string. Again, up from the bottom, over the straight stick, and down again.''

8. Add tail. That will cover
   end of stick one.

9. Punch two holes in the
   two squares on the kite.

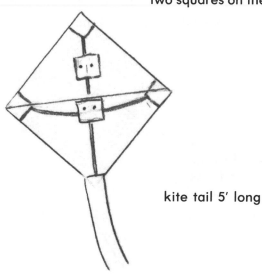

kite tail 5' long

"Finished, Teacher," Marcus said.

"Now," Mohan stated, "Take the ends of all the strings and tie them together into one big knot. Now tie the control string to the bow.

"Here is a strong, short stick. Start winding string around and around and around the stick, until this long piece—Marcus had about forty feet of string—is all wound on the stick. Then tie the end of the string on the stick to the knot on the kite that you made when you tied the four ends of string together.''

When the boys finished winding the string on the stick and tying the end of the string to the kite, Mohan said, ''Now it is completed, but we should

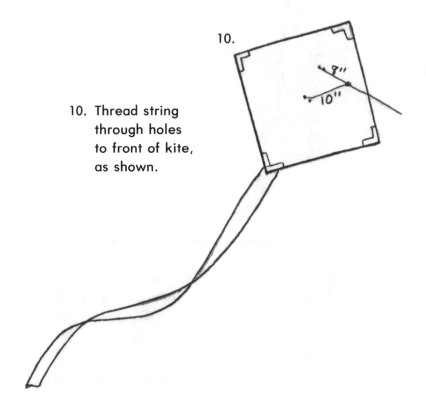

10. Thread string through holes to front of kite, as shown.

allow the glue to dry. We could carry the kite to your house so that your mother and father can see it. Then after lunch, it should be dry enough so that we can try it out.''

"Good idea. I'm sure my parents will be eager to see it," Marcus replied.

After Mohan had eaten his rice, he hurried to Marcus' house.

"Marcus," he called from the gate, "there is a breeze. I think the kite should sail really well. Have you finished your lunch?"

"Yes, I'll be right out," Marcus replied.

Marcus's mother came outside to watch the takeoff. She looked at Mohan and said, "Thank you, Mohan, for making this kite for Marcus. I hope you can have good times letting it fly."

"I believe it will go well today," Mohan answered her. "Now, Marcus, hang on to the string stick and start unwinding the string."

Up! Up! Up! went the kite.

"I will help you hang on," Mohan told him. "The kite really pulls with this breeze. Look how high it is. It is higher than the mango tree."

"There is a myna (mī nə) bird chasing it," Marcus's mother pointed out.

"This is great fun for us boys, but also for the birds," Marcus said. "Thank you, Mohan, for teaching me how to make a kite."

8.

Brothers

"Good morning, Mohan," Marcus greeted as he turned in at Mohan's gate. "You look sad this beautiful morning. Are you not feeling well?" he asked.

"I am quite well," Mohan answered, "but I have been thinking."

"That sounds good," Marcus returned. "That is what they say we are supposed to do in school, but it is good to do it other times too, I guess. Tell me the subject, and maybe I can help you think."

"Well," Mohan started slowly, "I have been thinking how nice it would be to have a brother. If I had a brother, he could help care for the animals. He could help carry water from the well. We could do lots of things together."

Mohan was sitting on a stone. He had his elbows on his knees and his chin propped in his hands.

Marcus went over and sat down beside him. He put his arm across Mohan's shoulder and said, "Mohan, I will be your brother."

"It won't work," Mohan replied.

"Why not?" Marcus asked.

"My skin is a different colour. Your skin is white and mine is brown, so I couldn't be your brother," Mohan said emphatically.

"I don't care about skin colour," Marcus assured him. "When we are together, I don't even think about it that our skins are different."

"I wonder why God made people with different colours of skin." Mohan was still thinking hard.

Marcus did not have an answer for that question. "Let us go and ask my father; he may know."

Off they went to Marcus's house.

"Father," Marcus began, "Mohan and I want to be brothers, but he says we can't be because our skins are different colours."

Mohan spoke next. "We are wondering why God made people's skin different colours. Marcus thought you could tell us."

"Well, now, let me think a little on that subject," Brother David said. "I will ask you a question first. Do you think the birds all wish they were one colour—the parrots and the peacocks, the sandpipers, the magpies, and the kingfishers? Suppose they all wanted to be green like the parrots. Or

suppose the flowers were all green like the grass. We enjoy seeing the different colours. I'm sure God enjoys seeing different colours of people. But do you know something? People are all the same inside.''

''But how do you know that?'' Mohan asked.

''The Bible says that God made people from every country of one blood,'' Brother David answered.

''You mean, then, that Marcus and I have the same kind of blood?'' Mohan could hardly believe his ears.

''Yes, Mohan, the same kind.'' Brother David continued, ''And best of all, God loves everybody. Marcus, let us sing, 'Jesus Loves the Little Children of the World,' for Mohan.''

Jesus loves the little children,
All the children of the world;
Red, brown, yellow, black, and white,
They are precious in His sight;
Jesus loves the little children of the world.

''I'm glad *brown* is in there,'' Mohan said. Just to make sure, he asked Brother David again, ''May Marcus and I be brothers? Of course, not in the same family, but just brothers?''

''That would be fine,'' Brother David answered.

''Thank you for explaining it to us,'' Mohan said. Then he added with a big smile, ''Come on, my new brother, Marcus, let's fly our kites. There is a good breeze out there.''

The boys soon had their kites flying high.

"This is great fun," Marcus said. "Mine is almost to the end of my string.''

"Hold on to it, Marcus," Mohan shouted. "I think the wind is changing its direction.''

Just then a strong gust of wind caught Marcus' kite and tangled it up in the big leaves of the coconut tree.

"What shall I do now?" Marcus asked.

"Hold on to your string, but don't tug at it or it may tear," Mohan instructed. "I will wind mine in; then I will try to help you. It surely pulls in hard with that strong breeze blowing.''

Mohan placed his kite flat on the ground and put a stone on top of it to keep it from blowing away.

"I will try to get it loose for you," Mohan offered. He wrapped his legs and arms around the trunk of the tree and pulled himself up by pushing his feet tightly against the trunk—almost as if he were walking.

"I think I can reach it if I stretch a little more," he called. "I have the string now. Up and over this leaf, and it is free.''

Just then a fresh breeze came, and the kite sailed into open space.

"Coming down the tree is almost more difficult

than going up,'' Mohan explained. ''If you don't keep your brakes on, you come too fast.''

''I am glad you are down safely,'' Marcus said. ''Thank you for getting my kite out of the tree. You are a real brother to me because that is the kind of deed brothers do for each other. They help each other when they are in trouble.''

''And when they are not in trouble,'' Mohan added. ''I will long remember this day because you helped me to know that skin colour doesn't matter and that we can be brothers.''

9.

A Visit to the Jungle

"Brother David invited us to go along to the jungle for a service tonight at Brother Mungal's (Mən gəl′) home," Father announced at breakfast time. Father and Mother had been going to the church services at Brother David's house. They had learned to love the Lord.

"Do you think we can go?" Mother asked. "It is quite far for Mohan to walk."

"I would really like to go," Mohan said.

"Maybe we could borrow a bicycle, or maybe Uncle Rojen would take us in his rickshaw," Mother suggested.

"That is a good idea," Father agreed.

At four o'clock, two rickshaws started out for the jungle village. In one rickshaw were Mohan and his father and mother. In the other rickshaw were Marcus and his father and mother.

"This is exciting," Marcus called to Mohan. "I have never been to the jungle. Will there be wild animals there?"

"We will need to wait and see, I guess. I am anxious to see Obhee (Ōb hē′). He is Brother Mungal's son," Mohan called back.

A Visit to the Jungle

Away they went. It almost looked as if they were racing. First Mohan's rickshaw was ahead, and then Marcus's rickshaw was ahead.

"Get out of the way!" Uncle Rojen yelled as he brought his rickshaw to a sudden halt. There was a large herd of cattle coming home from the pasture.

They started crossing the road in front of Uncle Rojen. He rang his rickshaw bell, but they did not hurry a bit.

Toot-toot-toooot! A bus had to wait too, and the driver was impatient.

Finally the last calf had crossed over, and they were on their way again.

"I wonder how far ahead Marcus is," Mohan said. "They just got past in time to miss that long wait."

Uncle Rojen pedaled very fast. They soon caught up with the other rickshaw.

"Are we almost there?" Marcus asked.

"We still have three miles to travel," Mohan's father answered. "Do you see all those banyan (ban′ yən) trees? That is the beginning of the jungle."

"I like the banyan trees. They make lots of shade with all the trees grown together," Marcus said. "Why are there so many trees all around the big one? They all seem to be joined at the top."

"The trees send down roots from their branches," Father explained. "When the roots reach the ground, they begin to grow a tree too, so they are joined at the top."

"I see Obhee coming to meet us!" Mohan exclaimed. "Namaste (Nə mə′ stā), Obhee," he called. (*Namaste* means "good morning" or "good-bye" in the language spoken in India.)

A Visit to the Jungle

"I am so happy to see you," Obhee greeted Mohan and Marcus as the rickshaws stopped at the gate. "Mother is preparing supper for you, and I am on my way to get banana plates. Would you like to come with me?" he invited.

"Oh, surely, that would be fun," Mohan answered.

"What are banana plates?" Marcus whispered his question to Mohan.

"They are banana leaves," Mohan explained. "People cut them in pieces and use them for plates. When the meal is over they give them to the goats. People eat the food and the goats eat the plates."

"The banana trees are over here beside the coconut trees," Obhee told them. He carefully cut a long, fresh, green leaf from one of the banana trees. It was six feet long.

"Would you like to drink some coconut milk?" Obhee asked.

"Yes. We would enjoy it," the boys agreed.

"If you will hold this banana leaf, Marcus," Obhee said, "I will climb up the coconut tree and cut some coconuts. Maybe your parents would like some too."

Up he scampered like a monkey.

"I couldn't do that," Marcus said. "You must do it very often to go so fast."

"I will throw some coconuts down. Are you

ready, Mohan? Here comes the first one.'' Obhee threw a nice, green coconut right into Mohan's arms.

''Here comes another—and another—and another,'' he said. Mohan had to hurry to put each coconut on the grass in time to catch the next one.

''We are getting quite a pile of them,'' Mohan called up to Obhee.

''One more—a big one for your father,'' Obhee said, laughing.

He scurried down the tree as fast as he had climbed up.

The boys made quite a procession as they walked home, led by Marcus waving the banana leaf like a banner. He was followed by Obhee and Mohan with their arms loaded with coconuts.

Brother Mungal cut the tops off the green coconuts with his sickle (a curved knife). He poked a hole in the end and gave one to each of the visitors.

''This is very refreshing,'' Brother David remarked.

''Yes, and it is healthy too,'' Brother Mungal added.

Obhee took a water pot and poured water over the guests' hands so that they would be clean for supper.

''Don't forget the rickshaw drivers,'' Brother Mungal reminded him. ''They will need supper too.''

Next Obhee put a piece of banana leaf in front of each of the guests who were seated on straw mats beside the house.

"Here is your banana plate, Marcus," Obhee chuckled.

Next, Obhee's mother brought a big kettle of rice and put a mound on each plate. Then she put a dip of dahl (däl) (similar to dried peas) over the rice.

"That looks good," Mohan said, "and I am really hungry."

"What is coming next?" Marcus whispered.

"It looks like curry. Yum, yum. I think it is egg curry, my favourite," Mohan told him.

When everyone was served, Brother David asked the blessing on the food.

Marcus watched how Mohan made little balls of rice with his hand and slipped them into his mouth. He tried to do it the same way.

"I'm so slow and sloppy," he told Mohan.

"Just use one hand," Mohan instructed him. "You need to keep one hand clean for passing things."

"Thank you for the tip," Marcus said.

When all had finished, Obhee passed a banana to each one. Next he came with the water pot so each could wash his hands if they were messy from eating.

"I will gather the plates and banana skins for the goats," Obhee told his mother.

"The village people are eager to have a service," Brother Mungal said. "I see some are coming already."

"Do you have a lantern?" Brother David asked. "It will soon be dark. It gets dark very quickly after sundown here in India."

"Yes, we will hang it on the tree here by the porch," Brother Mungal said.

Many neighbours came and sat on the straw mats in front of the porch. First they sang a number of songs, and then Brother David preached about the lost sheep.

Just as they were starting to sing the closing song, a cloud of insects flew in and swarmed around the lantern. People stopped singing because insects were everywhere. One flew into Mohan's mouth when he was singing. He spit it out. They crawled into the people's hair, on their arms, and in their ears. Brother David had a short closing prayer, and the people moved away from under the lantern.

"What are they?" Marcus asked.

"They are white ants," Mohan told him.

"I didn't know ants could fly; I thought they only crawled," Marcus said.

"Really, they are termites," Obhee added, "but

people call them white ants because they live in colonies like ants.''

''What are those shiny things on the ground under the lantern?'' Marcus asked.

''Those are the termites' wings,'' Mohan told him. ''They fly for only one trip; then their wings fall off. Do you see all those grub-like things wiggling around on the ground? They are the wingless termites.''

''Be careful, everyone,'' Brother Mungal warned. ''Here come the big, black, biting ants to eat up the white ants.''

Mother came and led Mohan and Marcus back from the light. People scrambled away in every direction because no one wanted to get bitten by a black ant.

''I will put out some insect dust to kill the ants,'' Brother Mungal said.

''It is time for us to go home,'' the visitors said. ''Thank you for the good supper and the fellowship.''

''Thank you for the banana plate and for teaching me about the white ants,'' Marcus told Obhee.

''Namaste, Obhee, and thank you,'' Mohan called from Uncle Rojen's rickshaw, all ready to start the ride back to his house.

10.

At the Seashore

"This is the day we go to the bay. This is the day we go to the bay," sang Mohan as he rolled up his straw mat that he had used for a bed. "I am so glad Father will take me along when he goes to the bay. I have always wanted to see the fishing boats," he told Mother.

"Father wants to go to the bay for some fish," Mother explained to Mohan.

"Is it far away?" Mohan asked.

"Yes, you will need to go on the bus," Mother told him.

"Oh, I am so happy. I have never had a bus ride." Mohan was so excited he could scarcely eat his rice.

"See you tonight, Mother," Mohan called over his shoulder as he walked with Father to the main road where the buses traveled.

"Here comes the bus," Mohan told Father.

"That one is going the wrong direction," Father explained. "If we got on that one we would end up very far away."

Mohan watched the other direction, and soon he saw a big green bus coming around the bend.

"That looks like the right one," Father said. He waved his handkerchief, and the bus driver slammed on the brakes.

They hurried to the door and were just inside when the bus started off with a big jerk. Mohan almost fell into the lap of a man sitting near the door.

"Move to the back!" the ticket man shouted. The aisle was full of people standing and holding onto poles. Father helped push Mohan through the crowd of people. He lifted him over boxes and bags that were piled in the aisle. Finally they reached the back. A man slid over on the bus seat and shared a small corner of the seat with Mohan.

Now the bus was stopping again. The man in front of Mohan stood up and started to push his way to the door. "You may have my seat," he told Father.

After jerking and bouncing along for what seemed like hours, they finally reached the city.

"At last," Mohan said as they got down from the bus.

"What is the name of the bay?" Mohan asked.

"It is the Bay of Bengal (Ben′ gôl)," Father told him, "and it is part of the Indian Ocean."

"Where do they get the fish?" Mohan asked next.

"Out of the waters in the bay. Men take their boats and nets and go away out where the water is deep," Father told him. "I think they will be starting to come in when we get there."

Already they could see the shining water.

"What is that black speck away out there?" Mohan asked, pointing to a speck on the horizon.

"That is a fishing boat, Son. Let us watch to see if it is coming in. If it gets bigger, that means it is coming closer," Father explained.

"I see more dots now," Mohan stated, "and I think they are coming closer."

"Now they look big," Father said awhile later. "They are stopping away out there because the water is too shallow to come in any closer."

"I see two men getting out of the first boat," Mohan announced. "They are bringing a stick. What are they going to do with it?"

"Just watch," Father told him. "See the big net of fish. They will put the stick through the net and put it over their shoulders. Then they will carry it in here to the shore."

"May I go out to meet them?" Mohan asked.

"Yes, that will be all right," Father replied.

At the Seashore

Since Mohan did not have shoes, he started running into the shallow water. Soon it came up to his knees.

"See, Father," he turned and called. "I am away out here."

Before long he met the two men carrying a big load of fish, and he turned around to follow them in to shore.

"Ouch!" Mohan cried.

The men stopped.

"Ouch!" Mohan screamed again.

Father heard Mohan and started running into the water. By the time Father reached him the tears were running down Mohan's cheeks. Mohan was a brave boy and scarcely ever cried, so Father knew there was something wrong. He picked up Mohan, and there was a big crab pinched onto Mohan's toe.

Immediately one of the fishermen squeezed the crab behind its head, and it let go of Mohan's toe.

"That feels better," said Mohan, smiling behind his tears.

Father carried Mohan in to the shore and set him down on the warm sand. By this time the fishermen had set down their heavy load of flip-flopping fish.

"Do you think your toe will need a bandage?" Father asked.

"It is bleeding a little," Mohan replied.

"I will put my handkerchief around it," Father

said. He wrapped the handkerchief neatly around Mohan's toe and tied it at the top.

"Look at all the loads of fish coming in," Mohan said excitedly. "There are little fish, big fish, and in-between sizes. What kind does Mother want?"

"She will want some little fish to salt and put in the sun to dry. She will want some of the in-between size to make fish curry for our supper. We will take some prawns (prô ns) home to keep alive until tomorrow. The prawns we will wrap in this seaweed to keep them cool. Here is a newspaper to put around the others. Then we will put them into these bags."

"Where will we eat our lunch?" Mohan asked.

"There is a nice shade tree by the main road. We could sit under it and watch for our bus," Father answered.

"Sounds like a good idea," Mohan said. "Shall I help carry the fish?"

"If you would carry the tiffan, that would help," Father answered.

Soon they were ready to eat. Mohan looked at his hands. "They are dirty," he said, "and they smell fishy."

"Run down to the water and wash them, but watch out for the crabs," Father warned.

Soon Mohan was back. They had just finished

eating their rice when the bus came along. They were able to find seats for the ride home.

Mohan soon fell asleep. When Father awakened him, they were almost to their road, and the bus was stopping.

"Shall I help carry the fish now?" Mohan asked.

"This bag is too heavy for you," Father said, "but you may carry the prawns if you wish." He gave Mohan the green seaweed package to carry.

Mother was happy to see them. She soon had a big kettle of fish curry bubbling.

"Um-m-m, it smells good," Mohan told her.

11.

An Early Morning Walk

"Tomorrow morning I must go to see Mr. Prakash (Prä käsh′) about buying one of the water buffaloes he has for sale," Father announced one evening after the family had finished eating their rice.

"May I go too? Please, may I go?" Mohan asked.

"We will need to go very early because Mr. Prakash goes out to his rubber plantation every morning to collect the latex. He goes out before the sun rises," Father told Mohan. Then he added, "Do you think you can be awake that early?"

"If Moorga doesn't call me early enough, please call me," Mohan said. "I think I had better go to bed right away."

The next morning as Father and Mohan were hurrying along, Mohan said, "It is still dark. Do you think we will get to Mr. Prakash's place in time to go out to his rubber trees with him?''

"It is quite a long way yet—about a mile farther," Father told him. "I hope we can be in time to go along with him."

"How do they use the rubber?" Mohan asked.

"They make tires for bicycles, rickshaws, and buses. They make sandals for people to wear and hoses for irrigating the crops, and they make many other things too."

"Does it grow on branches or is it in seeds or pods?" Mohan wondered.

"No, Son, it is under the bark," Father replied.

"How do they get it out?" Mohan asked next.

"If we are early enough, we can go with Mr. Prakash and watch him," Father told him.

"It is becoming light," Mohan said. "Would those tall trees far ahead be Mr. Prakash's rubber trees?" he asked.

Father stopped a moment to see where Mohan was pointing.

"Yes, I believe that is his place, and we will soon be there," Father decided. "We call the trees rubber trees, but their real name is hevea (hā′ vā ə) trees."

Father and Mohan walked very quickly. Mohan was too excited to think about getting tired.

"Good morning, Mr. Prakash," Father called

as they went through a gate and saw Mr. Prakash coming from his house.

"Good morning to you. What brought you out so early?" Mr. Prakash asked.

"We came over to see if you still have a water buffalo to sell. I will be needing one for ploughing when the rains start," Father told him.

"Yes, I have two I would sell. Come, you may take a look at them," Mr. Prakash said.

They walked out to the stable where the buffaloes were kept.

"The two at the end of the row are for sale," Mr. Prakash told Father. "They both have heavy horns, and the one has a white mark on his face."

Mohan hoped Father would choose the one with the white mark on his face. He would name him Star if Father liked the name because the white mark was like a star.

Father walked all around the animals. He felt their shoulders.

"They both have strong necks," he told Mr. Prakash. "I believe I will take this one—with the white face."

Mohan was very happy to hear that.

"Will it be all right if I come tomorrow afternoon to get him?" Father asked. "I will bring the rupees along."

"That is a deal," Mr. Prakash said. "Now I

must hurry to the rubber plantation. Do you want to come along?''

''We were hoping to,'' Father told him. ''Mohan has plenty of questions that need answers.''

''I'll see what kind of answers I can give. I hope the questions aren't too hard.'' Mr. Prakash smiled at Mohan.

''Why do you need to get out so early in the morning?'' Mohan asked first.

''That is because the sun would harden the latex, or milk, that comes out of the tree, so we need to get there before the sun gets too warm,'' Mr. Prakash explained.

''You will need to work quickly to get all these trees done before the sun gets warm,'' Mohan remarked.

''We only tap (cut) them every second day. This morning I will do the ones on the left side of this path, and tomorrow morning, the ones on the other side,'' Mr. Prakash told him.

''How tall are the trees?'' Mohan asked. ''They look as if they would touch the sky.''

Mr. Prakash laughed. ''No, they don't reach the sky, but they are about sixty or seventy feet high. Notice their long, slender trunks and light-coloured bark. Feel how smooth it is. Now we are ready for the first tree.''

Mohan squatted on his heels to watch.

"Do you see this brown material here in this groove in the bark? See how the groove comes around the tree like a spiral. Now watch what happens."

Mr. Prakash took hold of one end of the brown material and gave a jerk. A long, stretchy string came off.

"You may have this, Mohan. It stretches like a rubber band. Here is my 'gauge.' " Mr. Prakash showed Mohan a knife. "This is a special knife to cut a fresh groove right in the old one, but to cut a little deeper."

Mohan's eyes opened wide as he watched the cut being made.

"It looks like milk running down the little ditch. It is going into the coconut shell you have hung at the bottom of the groove!" he exclaimed.

"I must keep moving along," Mr. Prakash said. "The juice only runs about one-half hour. By the time I have the other trees cut this one will have stopped running for today. Then I will come back and begin here to gather the milk, or latex, that has come from the trees. I will empty the coconut shells into my bucket.

"The trees will seal themselves off when the milk stops flowing. In two days I will need to take out that brown rubber band and make a fresh cut, and the milk will flow again."

"What do you do with the milk, or latex?" Mohan asked.

"I will add some acid to it. That makes the rubber set. Then I will lift out the rubber and squeeze it and hang it up to dry," Mr. Prakash explained.

"We must go home," Father said, "so that Mr. Prakash can finish his work before the sun gets too hot. Thank you for taking time to explain to Mohan how we get rubber."

"Thank you very much, Mr. Prakash," Mohan said. "You are a very good teacher."

12.

Bringing

Home the Buffalo

"Marcus, let us hurry home so that we are there when Father comes with Star," Mohan urged. "I think he should be coming soon."

The boys climbed the bank from the river where they had been floating bark boats.

"Is that your new buffalo?" Marcus asked.

"Yes, Father said we may call him Star." Mohan talked fast because he was excited. "He is all black except for a white mark on his face that looks like a star. Do you think we could run?"

The boys ran until they reached Marcus's house. "I will ask Mother if I may come," Marcus said.

"Mother, may I go to Mohan's house to see Star?" Marcus asked.

"Well, Son, the stars aren't out in the daytime," his mother replied.

"Mohan's father is bringing him home this

afternoon.'' Then Marcus laughed. ''This Star is a buffalo. No wonder you didn't know what I was talking about. Star is his name.''

''Yes, you may go, but don't get in Star's way,'' his mother told him.

Marcus ran out to join Mohan.

''Mother didn't know what I was talking about when I asked if I could go to your place to see Star,'' Marcus told Mohan. ''She said you don't see stars in the daytime.''

The boys both laughed.

''But she understood when I told her that Star was a buffalo,'' Marcus added.

''Has Father come yet?'' Mohan asked his mother.

''Not yet,'' Mother told him. ''I have some coconut milk. Would you each like a drink?''

''Thank you, thank you,'' the boys said together.

''I never tasted coconut milk before I came to India,'' Marcus told them. ''I really enjoy it. It seems to cool you off on a hot day.''

Mother looked out the door and could see down the road. ''I see a buffalo coming and a man is following behind him carrying a stick,'' she announced.

''Hurrah!'' the boys shouted. They jumped up from the straw mat where they had been sitting. ''Let's go and meet them.''

By that time Star and Father were turning in at the gate.

Mohan was first, and he shouted, "Welcome to your new home, Star."

Star walked along, nodding his head up and down with each step, as if to say, "How do you do?"

"Hello, Star," Marcus began.

But as soon as Star caught sight of Marcus, he snorted. He turned around and started galloping off in the direction from which he had come.

"I'm sorry. What happened to him? What did I do?" Marcus asked, puzzled.

"I think he is afraid of your white skin," Father told him. "He has probably never seen a person with white skin before."

"What can we do?" the boys asked anxiously.

"I will try to catch him," Father said. "The speed he is traveling, he will probably be back at Mr. Prakash's place in a few minutes. See that cloud of dust away out there?"

"Yes," the boys replied.

"That is from Star kicking up his heels," Father told them. "When I bring him next time, Marcus had better stay in the house," Father advised. "It may take a day or two for Star to get acquainted with white skin."

Father turned and hurried back to Mr. Prakash's

place.

Just as the sun was going down, a tired Star followed by a very tired Father turned in at the gate.

"I took along that new rope that you wove from rice straw, Mother, so he was easy to handle coming home this time," Father said. "He was tired too from his extra run."

"Will you leave him tied all night?" Mohan asked.

"I think I will, and maybe tomorrow too until he gets acquainted with us and your friend," Father replied.

The next day Marcus came over and stood by the gate where he could see Star. The buffalo kept a wary watch on the boy and all his movements. Each day, Marcus came a little closer.

One day Marcus brought a surprise. He went toward Star. He talked quietly. "Namaste, Star," he said. "I have brought a surprise for you. It is behind my back."

Star moved back until the rope was tight. Then Marcus brought the big handful of green grass from behind his back and held it out toward Star.

Slowly the rope loosened and Star came a few steps forward. He reached out his long tongue for the tasty treat.

"That was a good idea," Mohan said. "Star is fond of nice green grass. I believe you will soon be able to pat him.''

Each day Marcus brought Star a handful of fresh green grass. One day when Star reached out his tongue for the grass, Marcus reached out his white hand and patted Star's head.

"That was a real victory," Mohan's father told Marcus. "You won Star by kindness. Someday when we are ploughing Star will let you ride on his back."

"That will be a happy day," Marcus replied.

13.

The Monsoons Arrive

"I think the rains will start any day now," Father told Mother one morning. "I was talking to the village men last evening, and they are sure that they will come very soon."

"We have our rice seed ready to plant in the seedling plot as soon as we know the rains are starting," Mother said.

Mohan sat listening and thinking. "It has been a long time since we had any rain," he said. "The cattle will be glad for plenty of water and fresh grass. It is very dry and dusty."

"Yes, it is almost nine months since the last rains," Father remembered. "There have been some years when we didn't get enough rain to raise our rice crop. Then there was famine. People were hungry. We ate leaves from the trees. There wasn't grass or food for the animals. It was very bad."

"Should we pray that the rains would come this year?" Mohan asked. "And that there will be enough?"

"Yes, Mother and I have already been praying for that," Father told him. "It is already June 14, so by the end of this week, I believe the monsoons (mon sōōnz′) will have started."

"Why are they called monsoons?" Mohan asked.

"Really, the monsoons are winds," Father explained. "In the hot season the wind blows from the ocean to the land. In the winter it changes direction and blows from the land to the ocean. In the summer as the wind blows across the ocean it takes up moisture. Then later, this moisture falls as rain. We call these the 'wet monsoons' or the 'rainy season.' "

That very day, Mohan and Marcus were out playing with the goats and their little kids.

"Look, Marcus, they are coming," Mohan called, looking toward the east.

"Who is coming?" Marcus asked.

"The monsoons," Mohan told him.

"Who are they anyway, your cousins?" Marcus asked.

"No, Marcus, it is the rain that we have been waiting for," explained Mohan.

Just then a gust of wind and dust swished past

the boys.

"Look at those dark clouds churning in the sky, and look at those little whirlwinds sucking up dust. See how the air is brown with dust." Mohan showed Marcus.

Next there was a flash of lightning and a crash of thunder.

"I think I had better run home," Marcus said, "but that wind is so strong I don't know if I can walk into it."

"I will go with you," Mohan said. He took Marcus by the arm.

The boys struggled up the road toward Marcus's house.

"What is that?" shouted Marcus above the whining of the wind.

"That is some thatch blowing off Sosan's house roof," Mohan shouted back.

"How will you get home?" Marcus shouted again.

"No problem," Mohan assured him. "The wind will be on my back and will blow me home. I will just need to get stopped at the right place."

"Thank you for helping me home," Marcus said. "I hope you will be all right."

Flash! *Crash*!

Off Mohan went on the run, almost carried by the wind.

The Monsoons Arrive

"There goes more of Sosan's roof," Mohan said to himself as palm leaves mixed with dust went whirling past him. "And I think I see our roof lifting."

Mohan's feet flew, as he was nearly carried by the wind.

"Mohan," called a familiar voice.

There was Mother running to meet him. She put her arm around him, and together they ran home.

"I am glad you are all right. That wind is really strong. I could hardly see you for the dust in the air," Mother told him.

Just as they turned in at their gate, great drops of rain fell.

"Thank God," Mother said.

As they entered their house, the rain started to fall very fast. There was a strong gust of wind, and the thatch over their heads started to blow off, leaf by leaf. Soon rain was coming into the house.

"Oh! What will we do? Where will we sleep?" Mohan asked.

"Don't worry, Son," Mother comforted him. "Father will soon be here, and he will know what to do. There always is a bad storm with strong winds when the rains start."

Soon Father came running into the house. "Is everyone all right?" he asked. "This surely is a hard storm. Dust, dust, dust, blowing everywhere. I could hardly see to tie up the animals. It looks as if we will get a good rain tonight. What's going on in the corner here?''

Mother answered, ''I am afraid the thatch on that corner of the roof has blown off. The rain is coming in.''

''I thought I had it all tied tightly, but with that strong wind I will not be surprised if we lose part of it,'' Father said.

''I hope the rest stays on,'' Mohan added. ''It is dripping right where I sleep.''

''We can easily move your straw mat to another place,'' Mother assured him. Then turning to Father she asked, ''But how can we fix that hole for tonight? It will probably rain all night.''

''I have that piece of plastic that blew here last year in the monsoon storm,'' Father told them. ''I can put that on the underside of the roof for tonight. Maybe tomorrow it will stop raining long enough for me to patch the roof on the outside.''

''God answered our prayers! The monsoons have started,'' Mother said. ''I believe He will send us good rains this year.''

''I will help pray for them too,'' Mohan promised.

14.

Planting Rice

"Mother," Mohan called as he came running through the gate, "guess where I have been."

"To China," Mother guessed. "I know you can run very fast."

"Oh, Mother, not that far." Mohan laughed. "I was down to the plot where you have sown the rice for the little seedlings. Can you guess what I saw?"

"A tiger?" Mother guessed, with a twinkle in her eye.

Mohan laughed again. He enjoyed playing the guessing game with Mother. "No," he told her, "it was not a tiger nor an elephant nor a jackal. They were small and green."

"Lizards?" she guessed.

"No, not lizards," Mohan answered.

"Frogs?" She tried again.

"No, not frogs. Do you give up?" Mohan asked.

"All right. What did you see?" Mother asked.

"The rice you planted is growing, and it is as high as this." Mohan held his finger and thumb as far apart as he could get them.

"Now can you guess what we will be doing next week?" Mother asked him.

"Going to China?" Mohan guessed with a mischievous look on his face.

"Not that far," Mother told him.

"To Uncle Rojens?" He tried again.

"No, not that far. Do you give up?" Mother asked.

"Yes, please tell me," Mohan answered.

"Well, first of all we will go to the plot where the rice is growing," Mother explained. "We will pull the little seedlings, or plants, and tie them into bunches. Then you and Sosan will carry them in your jhilgis (jil′ kēz) to where Sosan's mother and I will be planting them."

"Sounds like fun," Mohan remarked, "but what if it rains?"

"We will do as they do in China when it rains," Mother told him.

"What is that?" Mohan asked.

"Why don't you ask Father when he comes?" Mother suggested.

108

Planting Rice

That evening Mohan met Father at the gate.

"I have a question for you, Father," he began. "What do they do in China when it rains?"

"Let's go ask Mother," Father said. "Mother, Mohan is asking what they do in China when it rains."

"Well," Mother began slowly, "they just let it rain."

"That is what we do too," Father said, "and we are thankful for every drop, especially now that rice transplanting time is so near."

"How are you getting along working the plots?" Mother inquired.

"I think we will be ready to start transplanting next week," Father told her.

Mohan could hardly wait. If he could carry bunches of seedlings in his jhilgi, he must surely be getting big.

Monday finally came. Mother and Mohan went to the rice plot.

"There is Father ploughing," Mohan said. "He must have gone to the plot very early."

"Yes. He went before daylight," Mother told him. "He will soon have the first one ready for us."

"I never can understand how he knows where he is ploughing when the water is on top of the ground like that," Mohan said.

"He ploughs one way first, and then he ploughs

the field crosswise. The reason is to mix the water into the ground. That leaves it like thick soup. Then we place the little rice plants in the muck,'' Mother explained. ''We had better hurry and begin pulling seedlings,'' she added. ''Here come Sosan and his mother to help.''

Mother showed Mohan how to hold the pulled plants in one hand and wrap a piece of grass around them. ''Now tie a knot in the grass and lay the bunch in your jhilgi,'' Mother instructed him.

They worked quickly and soon had the jhilgis filled.

''I see Father has moved to the next plot, so we can start to plant. Mohan, if you will drop your little bunches along the row beside me and Sosan drop his beside his mother's row, then we will plant while you and Sosan pull and bunch and carry another load,'' Mother directed.

Soon the boys came again with their loads.

''You are just in time,'' Mother told them. ''See, we have only a few more left to plant.''

The boys quickly set their bunches of rice plants off and ran back for another load.

''This is fun,'' Mohan said. ''Do you think we can keep up with them?''

''We will need to hurry,'' Sosan replied, ''but I think we can do it.''

Back and forth the boys ran. The mothers sang

as they backed across the plot, planting the seedlings in nice, straight rows. Mohan and Sosan soon joined the song.

By lunch time the plot was finished.

"The work has gone well," Mother said. "By tomorrow morning, Father should have the next plot ready to plant."

On the walk back to the house, Mohan said to Sosan, "Work seems to go easy if we sing."

"Yes," Sosan agreed. "I don't even feel tired."

"See you in the morning," Mohan called as he turned in at his gate.

15.

Mohan and the

Goat Herder

"Sosan asked me to go along with him tomorrow to herd the goats," Mohan called to Mother as he was going down the path to his house. "May I, please, Mother? May I, please?"

"We will see what Father says," Mother answered.

Several weeks had passed since all the little rice plants had been planted. The rice fields looked green and beautiful.

"I think it would be time for you to learn how to herd goats," Father agreed. "Sometime you may need to go every day. But you will have to wake up very early in the morning," he warned.

"I will try to sleep fast so that I am done in time," Mohan said as he got his straw mat and spread it on the floor in the corner.

Just as the sun was waking up, Mother put rice

in Mohan's tiffan. She shook him awake and gave him his bowl of rice for breakfast.

Soon he heard Sosan coming down the road. He was gathering goats from each house in the village. He was taking them out to pasture.

Mohan chased Nanny, Buckree (Buk′ rē), and Meena (Mē′ nä) from their pen beside the house. "Here we come," Mohan called as they joined the goats and Sosan.

When they came to the edge of the village, they stopped to count the goats. "Sixty-seven is correct," Sosan counted.

The boys chased the goats uphill and downhill, following paths and trails. Finally, Sosan said, "Look, Mohan, do you see those tall banyan trees? That is where the goats will stop today. It is shady, and there is a little pool of water where they will drink."

"Are we nearly there? My legs are getting a little tired," Mohan replied.

Finally they reached the spot. Mohan stretched himself under the trees and looked through the leaves at the blue, blue sky.

Suddenly Mohan sat up and asked, "What are those dark brown things hanging in the tree?"

Sosan looked up and laughed. "Those are kabodhis (kə bōd′ hē). They are bat-like creatures. They can stay all day upside-down, hanging on by

their feet.''

"They hang there like worm nests,'' Mohan added. "There must be a hundred of them.''

"They stay together in big flocks,'' Sosan told him.

"There they go. We must have frightened them,'' Mohan shouted. "Look how big their wings are. They look like kites as they sail up into the sky.''

"Yes,'' Sosan told him, "their wings measure about a metre from tip to tip. Something strange about them is that they will not drink water from a puddle or stream. They hang upside-down, and when it rains they turn up their heads and open their mouths and let the raindrops fall in.''

"I wonder what they do in the dry season when it doesn't rain.'' Mohan was puzzled. "I think I would get really thirsty.''

"I would too,'' Sosan agreed. "One thing more about them—when people are sick, someone will shoot a kabodhi and prepare it for the sick person. It helps him become well. We had better go now and check on the goats to be sure they are not in somebody's rice field.''

Off the boys went and found the goats behaving very well. They were walking along the edges of the rice fields, eating grass and weeds. Mohan gave Nanny, Buckree, and Meena each a loving pat.

"I am starting to feel a little hungry," Mohan informed Sosan.

"I will show you how to tell when it is dinner time," Sosan told him. "Do you remember that when we left home this morning the sun was over there?" Sosan pointed to the east. "It was just above the trees. Then it was eight o'clock. Now it is almost above our heads, so it is eleven-thirty. When it is straight above our heads, and there are no shadows in front or behind us, then it will be twelve o'clock. We can soon eat our dinner."

Mohan was very happy with the thought of dinner.

"When the sun is on that side of the sky," Sosan continued, pointing to the west, "and the shadows are tall behind us, then it will be four o'clock and time to go home."

"Father says the sun is God's clock," Mohan told Sosan.

When the sun was straight above them, the boys bowed their heads and thanked God for their food. They opened their tiffans and ate their rice. Then they stretched out under a banyan tree for a little rest.

"Do you know how to play the stone game?" Sosan asked Mohan.

"I have watched you older boys play, but I have never played it," Mohan answered.

"Come over here to this sandy spot, and I will

teach you," Sosan suggested. "Will you bring me a handful of little stones?"

"Yes, I will get the stones," Mohan gladly consented. He hurried to gather the stones.

By the time Mohan got over to Sosan, he found him marking squares in the sand with a stick.

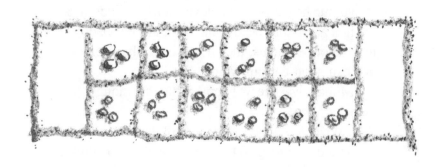

"Now, put three stones into each square. This will be your side, and that will be mine," Sosan directed. "Now, to show you how, I will start. I will pick up the three stones from one of my squares and drop one in each of the next three squares on the right side, like this. If I end up with my last stone of the three in the big end section, I can have another turn right away. Now you may do the same."

Mohan picked up three from his side and did the same.

Next, Sosan took the stones from a square that had four in it. This time he put one stone in the end section and one in three of Mohan's spaces.

"Ha, ha, ha," Mohan laughed. "You surprised me."

"The winner is the one who gets all the stones out of his squares first," Sosan explained.

"I am sure that you will win," Mohan said, "but this is a nice game, and I want to learn to play it well."

The boys played game after game. Soon Mohan was the winner. They had started the next game when suddenly there was a loud yell.

"Sosan, what are you doing?"

The boys stopped the game and jumped up. There was Garibsai (Gə rib′ sī) standing on the edge of his rice field with a stick in his hand. Sosan trembled as he ran over to Garibsai.

"Your goats are getting into my rice field," Garibsai shouted, shaking his stick at the frightened boys.

"I'm very sorry," Sosan said. "I'll try to watch them better tomorrow. It is time we start back for the village."

"Be sure to keep them out of my rice field," Garibsai shouted after them, still shaking his stick.

The boys started for home, following the goats.

Mohan said, "Thank you, Sosan, for bringing me along and teaching me the stone game. I was scared when Garibsai yelled at us, weren't you?"

"I was a little," Sosan told him. "I am glad he didn't chase us. I really am sorry that I didn't watch the goats better. I was having such a good time playing "stone" that I forgot about them. But that is no excuse. I will try to watch the goats better tomorrow."

16.

Mohan Goes to School

"Tomorrow is the day. Tomorrow is the day. Tomorrow is the day," sang Mohan as he helped Mother gather the plates after a big supper of rice.

"What day is tomorrow?" teased Mother. "Is it market day, or is it Sunday or your birthday?"

"Oh, Mother, did you forget? Tomorrow I go to school. Tomorrow I go to school. I just can't wait, Mother. I just can't wait," Mohan told her.

"What are you going to do about it?" Mother asked.

"I guess just go to bed and sleep" was Mohan's answer.

Before he spread out his mat for sleeping, he again got out his slate and slate pencil and his tiffan for his rice. His new shirt was ready, waiting for him.

Ur-ur-aroo! crowed Moorga. *Ur-ur-aroo!*

Mohan woke up with a start. He thought this morning that Moorga was saying, "Off to school. Off to school."

He ran to the river for a bath. When he got back to the house, Mother combed his hair and buttoned his shirt. He got a neemwood (nēm' wood) stick. He chewed one end fine and brushed his teeth.

By that time Mother called, "Mohan, your rice is ready."

Mohan got his bowl and sat on the straw mat beside Father.

When Father thanked God for the food, he added a special prayer for Mohan. "Dear God," he prayed, "be with Mohan as he goes to school. Thank You for a Christian school and teacher. Help him to learn to read so that he can read the Bible to Mother and me. Help him to obey his teacher. Please keep him safe from harm and danger. In Jesus' Name. Amen."

Mohan carried his slate and pencil and went up the street to meet Marcus. Marcus was ready to go to school.

"Do you have your slate and pencil?" Mohan checked.

"Yes. Do you have your tiffan?" Marcus asked.

"No, I forgot it," Mohan answered. "I must run home and get it, or I will be hungry."

"I will go with you," Marcus said, and they

hurried back to Mohan's house for his tiffan.

When they got to school, the teacher was ringing the bell. The bell was a long piece of iron, hanging from the branch of a tree. He hit it with a hammer.

"That means we need to stand in straight rows," a big boy told the two little boys. "Then we will go inside."

"All those who are at school for the first time, stand on this side," the teacher said.

Mohan and Marcus stood by the other boys until all were in nice, straight rows.

"The new pupils may come in first," the teacher instructed.

The boys walked into the school, following the teacher. The older pupils came last of all.

"You may sit on this straw mat here," the boys were told next. "Make two straight rows. That is right.

"First I will print your names at the tops of your slates," the teacher told the new pupils. "You may print them underneath. In India you must learn two languages, so I will print them in English letters first and then in Hindi (Hin' dē)."

The boys worked hard and long.

Mohan and Marcus watched the teacher carefully write their names on their slates. He wrote them first in English and then in Hindi, like this:

Marcus मार्कस

Mohan मोहन

"Time to eat your lunch," the teacher said.

After the teacher asked the blessing, Mohan and Marcus hurried outdoors and sat under a mango tree. As they ate their food, the boys talked about school.

"Why are there only boys coming to school?" Marcus asked.

"I think it is because most girls don't go to school at all," Mohan answered. "Maybe in the cities some girls go to school, but here in our village they need to stay at home to help herd the cattle and look after their little brothers and sisters while their mothers work in the fields. Neither my mother nor my father can read. They want me to go to school so that I can read to them. Father can write his name, but Mother cannot."

"If we try really hard, we should soon know how to write our names," Marcus decided.

"The bell is ringing," the boys said at the same time.

Together they ran and stood in their line again.

In the afternoon the teacher put the numbers 1, 2, and 3 on their slates, and they learned how to make them.

Before they went home, the teacher said, "Now write your names again in English and in Hindi to take home and show your parents."

Mohan tried his best and he wrote:

Mohan मोहन

Marcus tried hard to write his name:

Marcuz मारकुन

"I have trouble getting the N straight," Mohan said on the way home.

"And I have trouble with the S," Marcus said. "He is such a twisty fellow, I don't know when I have him standing on his head or on his feet."

"Maybe tomorrow we will get them straight," Mohan said as they parted.

17.

The Telltale Trail

"The rice is all carried in, and we have a large stack of sheaves," Father announced one evening when Mother was preparing supper.

"That is wonderful," Mother replied. "When will we start threshing?"

"I think I would be ready to start tonight," Father answered, "if it would suit you to help me. I will need you to keep the straw pushed into the centre with a stick."

"Yes, I could help," Mother replied.

"May I help too, Father?" Mohan asked. "I hope I may. Why do you work at night?"

"It is cooler for the oxen," Father explained. "You remember how they walk around and around and around on the pile of sheaves. That tramps out the kernels of rice."

"Yes," Mohan added, "the oxen are all tied

together—six or eight of them—and you use your ox goad to drive them. That is what you call the sharp stick, is it not?"

"That is right," Father replied. "You may help awhile, but then my boy must get some sleep so that he can go to school tomorrow."

"Supper is ready," Mother said as she gave them each a bowl of steaming rice and sat on the straw mat beside Mohan.

Father gave thanks for the food, and then they used their clean fingers and made little bite-sized balls of rice and popped them into their mouths.

"Thank you for the good supper," Father and Mohan said together. Then they went out to the threshing floor behind the house.

Just that very day Mother had swept the large patch of ground—the threshing floor—with her little broom made from veins of the coconut palm leaves. Then all over the spot, she spread cow dung thinned with water. It baked hard from the hot sun and left a nice, smooth finish.

"Mother worked hard to get this place ready today. Would you like to help me spread the sheaves of rice in a big circle like this?" Father asked Mohan as he took a big armful and began to make a fluffy pile.

Soon Mother came to join them.

"That looks so soft I feel like jumping into it,"

Mohan exclaimed.

"You may jump into it all you wish," Father replied. "What you shell out the oxen won't need to. We must make the pile a bit deeper."

The three worked together for some time and then Father and Mother stood back and looked at what they had done.

"It is deep enough," Father said, "but it is not quite round. We don't want the oxen to miss any."

"Could Mohan and I finish the pile while you get the oxen ready?" Mother asked.

"That would save some time," Father agreed.

Mohan and Mother made a nice circle and then added a few more armfuls of sheaves.

"It is almost as high as my head," Mohan decided.

"That looks just right," Father said when he came back with the oxen. "I think we should be able to get this pile all threshed tonight. There is a big moon coming up, so we won't need a lantern."

Father tied the six oxen together. "Birch, birch, birch," he called, and the oxen started their long walk. Around and around and around they went.

"It almost makes me dizzy to watch them," Mohan said after a while.

Soon Mohan yawned sleepily. "I think I am ready to go to bed," he told Mother. "I can find my straw mat and blanket, so you won't need to

come in.''

"Good night, Son," Mother replied. "May the angels watch over you while you sleep. Father and I will be out here for a few hours yet."

Father and Mother kept working together, Father chasing the oxen around the circle and Mother pushing in the loose stalks of rice so that none of the precious grain would be missed.

Four hours later Father called to his tired wife, "Mother, that is it for tonight. I will tie the oxen and then come out to help gather the straw off the grains and sweep the grain onto a pile. I believe I should sleep out beside the grain on a straw mat. Last year we had some grain stolen. We can't afford that again this year."

Weary Father tied the animals in the stalls. Then he filled the mangers with freshly threshed rice straw. Mother drew water from the well and gave the oxen water to drink.

"We will stack the straw on this side of the threshing floor," Father said.

Together they carried big armfuls of the fluffy straw and soon had a large heap.

"It looks soft like a cloud," Father remarked. "Maybe I will just sleep on that for the rest of the night."

They swept the shelled grains of rice onto a pile.

"That looks great for the first night's

threshing,'' Father rejoiced.

"Yes, we surely have much to thank God for. He has been good to us,'' Mother replied. As she turned to go into the house, she called over her shoulder. "You had better sleep with one eye open tonight, in case you get visitors.''

Father snuggled down into the pile of rice straw and was soon in a deep sleep. He dreamed he was walking around and around following the oxen.

Ur-ur-aroo, crowed Moorga close to Father's head.

Father jumped with a start. "Where am I? Why am I out in the straw? Where is Mother? Where is Mohan?'' These questions pushed into his mind. Then he remembered and started to laugh.

"Good morning, Father,'' Mohan greeted him. "Did you get some sleep? I'm sure you are tired. Mother said you slept out here all night. You got a nice big pile of grain.''

By this time Father joined Mohan, and they walked around the newly threshed pile of grain. Then Father blinked.

"Are those footprints on the edge of the pile?'' he asked. "Did I sleep so soundly that someone came and I didn't hear him? I wonder which way he went!''

"Look, Father.'' Mohan pointed excitedly. "See this little trail of rice? I wonder where it will

stop."

"That is a good clue," said Father. "We will follow it and find out. Whoever it was must have had a bag with a hole in it."

It was an easy matter to follow the trail of rice—around the corner and over the hill.

"It turns in at Cheena's (Chē′ nə) house, I see," Father said.

Knock! Knock! Knock! Cheena was awakened from a troubled sleep.

"Come in," he called sleepily, expecting to see his brother.

There stood Father and Mohan. What could Cheena say? He was caught. There on the floor was the bag of stolen rice. Father looked at Cheena. Cheena flinched and looked at the floor, then at Father, and then at the floor again.

Finally he spoke. "You know I am caught. I am

very sorry. Can you forgive me? Here is your rice, but how did you find me?''

Father smiled. ''Ah, Cheena, you left a good trail. Check your bag for holes next time. But, Cheena, it is wrong to steal. Don't let there be a next time.''

''I want this time to be the last,'' Cheena answered soberly. ''Here are some rupees to pay for the rice that was wasted.''

''Cheena,'' Father said, ''since Brother David came, he has been teaching us about the Bible. I have learned a short verse that God spoke. It is, 'Thou shalt not steal.' I have also been thinking about your little Sameel (Säm′ ē əl) and Santosie (Sän tō′ sē). You don't want them to grow up to be thieves, do you, Cheena?''

Cheena shook his head no.

''Then why don't you ask Jesus to come into your life and save you from your sins?'' Father pled.

''I will go right away this morning and talk with Brother David,'' Cheena replied.

As Father and Mohan walked toward home, Mohan said, ''Father, I'm glad you told Cheena what the Bible says about stealing. I hope he never steals anything again.''

''We must pray for him,'' Father's replied.

18.

Uncle Purno

"Marcus, would you come with me?" Mohan called as he hurried down the street.

"I will ask my mother, but where are you going?" Marcus replied.

"Mother asked me to take some bananas and a bag of rice to Uncle Purno (Pūr′ nō)," Mohan told him.

"Where does he live?" Marcus asked.

"He lives outside the village in that little mud hut among the mango trees," Mohan replied.

Marcus joined Mohan after his mother had said yes.

"And you say he is your uncle?" Marcus questioned.

"Well, he is not really my uncle," Mohan explained, "but in India we call older men Uncle and older ladies Auntie. Mother and Father say that it shows spect for them. I don't mean spect, I mean respect. If I would not call Uncle Purno Uncle, I would be punished.''

''I hope I can remember to always do that too,'' Marcus decided, ''because I want to show spect . . . or . . . or . . . respect too.''

''Uncle Purno is a leper,'' Mohan shared.

''A what?'' Marcus asked.

''He is a leper. He had that bad sickness called leprosy, but he is better now,'' Mohan explained. ''But he cannot work and is very poor.''

''Well, if he is better, why can't he work?'' Marcus reasoned.

''Because he has no fingers or toes,'' Mohan explained. ''They fell off because of his sickness. Because he is so poor, people sometimes send him food. Do you see the house in that cluster of trees? That is Uncle Purno's place.''

''It surely looks small,'' Marcus commented.

The boys called from the path, ''Namaste, Uncle Purno.''

''Come in,'' came a voice. Then a tall, thin man appeared. He needed to bend over to come outside because the doorway was quite low.

''Well, well, well! I certainly am glad to see you,'' the man said. ''Come, let us sit under this tree and chat awhile. Who is your friend, Mohan?''

''This is Marcus. His father is Brother David.

He is our minister.'' Mohan introduced Marcus.

"I am glad to meet you, Uncle Purno,'' Marcus said. "I am sure my father would like to meet you too. I will tell him where you live.''

"I hope I am at home when he comes,'' Uncle Purno told him. "Since I lost my fingers and toes, and I cannot work, I go to the city. There people give money and food. I have this tin cup. I hold it out to people and they put things in it—sometimes a rupee. I often sing. People know me by my song.''

"Oh, I almost forgot. Uncle Purno, Mother sent some rice and bananas for you. Now you won't need to beg tomorrow,'' Mohan told him.

"Oh, thank you, thank you. Your mother is very kind. Please tell her 'thank you.' '' Uncle Purno said gratefully.

"How long have you had this sickness?'' Marcus asked.

"Since I was fifteen years old. I lived with my parents and brothers and sister. We don't know where I got it, but two white spots showed on my foot. You can easily see white spots on brown skin. I tried to hide them, but one day my mother saw them. She called the witch doctor from the next village,'' Uncle Purno explained.

"What kind of doctor is that?'' Mohan asked.

"It is one who uses all sorts of things for cures,'' Uncle Purno answered. "He found a piece of rubber

and burned it. Then he took the ashes from it and put them on a stick. Next he rubbed and rubbed it into the spots until they started to bleed.''

The boys got tears in their eyes, so Uncle Purno changed the subject.

"For years I had to live away from home," he continued, "so that I wouldn't spread the disease to my family. One day I was walking in the city when a real doctor saw me. He took me to a hospital. By this time, my toes and fingers had fallen off. At the hospital they had pills and medicine that stopped the disease.''

"How long were you in the hospital?'' Mohan asked.

"I was there for five years" was the answer. "It was a special hospital for people with leprosy. Finally the doctor said I was cured and could leave.''

"I am so glad you can be out of the hospital,'' Mohan told him.

"Thank you for telling us about the disease, and especially that you are better,'' Marcus said. "My father reads from the Bible about Jesus making ten men well. They had leprosy too.''

"Would your father come and read me that story sometime?'' Uncle Purno asked.

"I am sure he would be happy to do that,'' Marcus told him.

"Namaste, Uncle Purno,'' Mohan said. "We

hope to see you again.''

"Please do come back," Uncle Purno invited. "Thank your mother for the rice and bananas. Namaste to you both.''

Mohan and Marcus waved to Uncle Purno and then walked down the road together.

Glossary of Pronunciations
and Definitions

1. Baboo (Bä boo')
2. banyan (ban' yən) *a fig tree*
3. Barda Baboo (Bär' da Bä boo')
4. Bay of Bengal (Bā of Ben' gôl)
5. Binode (Bi nōd)
6. Brother Mungal (Brother Mən gəl')
7. Buckree (Buk' rē)
8. Cheena (Chē' nə)
9. Chota Baboo (Chō' ta Bä boo')
10. dahl (däl) *a vegetable similar to dried peas*
11. Garibsai (Gə rib' sī)
12. Garum Chai (Gər əm Chä' ē) *hot tea*
13. hevea (Hā' vā ə) *a tree that produces sap from which rubber is made*
14. Hindi (Hin' dē) *the language spoken in India*
15. Jay Prakash (Jī-ē Prä käsh')
16. jhilgi (jil' kē) *a pair of baskets carried across the shoulders*
17. Kabodhi (kə bōd' hē) *a bat-like creature*
18. Mahesh (Mə häsh')
19. mango (mang' gō) *an Indian fruit*

20. Meena (Mē nä)
21. metre (mē′ tər) *a measure about 39 inches*
22. Mohan (Mō′ han)
23. monsoons (mon so͞onz) *a name for special winds*
24. Moorga (Mo͞or′ gä)
25. Moorgee (Mo͞or′ gē)
26. Munci (Mən′ sē)
27. Mungal (Brother) (Mən gəl′)
28. myna (mī′ nə) *a kind of bird*
29. namaste (nə mə′ stä) *a greeting meaning hello and good-bye*
30. neemwood (nēm′ wood) *a kind of tree*
31. Nehru (Nē hə ro͞o′)
32. Obhee (Ōb hē′)
33. Prakash (Mr.) (Prä käsh′)
34. prawns (prôns) *a kind of fish*
35. Purno (Uncle) (Pūr′ nō)
36. Rao (Rä′ ō)
37. rickshaw (rik′ shô) *a three-wheeled bicycle-type cart*
38. Rojen (Uncle) (Rä′ jən)
39. rupee (ro͞o′ pē) *money used in India*
40. Sameel (Säm′ ē əl)
41. Santosie (Sän tō′ sē)

42. scarab (scar′ əb) *a large beetle*
43. Sosan (Sō′ sän)
44. supa (sū′ pä) *a rice-straw pan for cleaning rice*
45. thatch *a palm-leaf roof*
46. tiffan (tif′ fən) *basket for lunch*